Story and Pictures by
TOMIE DE PAOLA

ANDY
(THAT'S MY NAME)

SIMON & SCHUSTER BOOKS FOR YOUNG READERS

New York London Toronto Sydney New Delhi

SIMON & SCHUSTER BOOKS FOR YOUNG READERS
An imprint of Simon & Schuster Children's Publishing Division
1230 Avenue of the Americas, New York, New York 10020
Copyright © 1973 by Tomie dePaola
SIMON & SCHUSTER BOOKS FOR YOUNG READERS is a trademark of Simon & Schuster, Inc.
For information about special discounts for bulk purchases, please contact Simon & Schuster Special Sales at 1-866-506-1949
or business@simonandschuster.com.
The Simon & Schuster Speakers Bureau can bring authors to your live event. For more information or to book an event,
contact the Simon & Schuster Speakers Bureau at 1-866-248-3049 or visit our website at www.simonspeakers.com.
Book design by Tomie dePaola and Laurent Linn
The text for this book is hand lettered.
The illustrations for this book are rendered in pen and ink line with black wash and two-color separations.
Manufactured in China
1017 SCP
This Simon & Schuster Books for Young Readers hardcover edition October 2015
2 4 6 8 10 9 7 5 3
The Library of Congress has catalogued a previous edition as follows:
dePaola, Thomas Anthony. Andy: that's my name.
Summary: Andy's friends construct different words from his name: "an" words, "and" words, and "andy" words.
I. Title. PZ7.D439An [E] 73-4593
ISBN 978-1-4814-4233-6
ISBN 978-1-4814-4554-2 (eBook)